Dear Family and Friends of N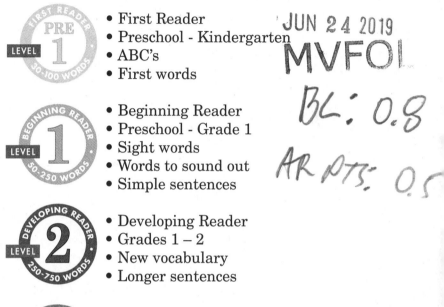

Welcome to Scholastic Reader. We ... ty years of experience with teachers, ... put it into a program that is designed to match your child's interest and skills. Each Scholastic Reader is designed to support your child's efforts to learn how to read at every age and every stage.

LEVEL PRE 1 — *FIRST READER · 50-100 WORDS*
- First Reader
- Preschool - Kindergarten
- ABC's
- First words

LEVEL 1 — *BEGINNING READER · 50-250 WORDS*
- Beginning Reader
- Preschool - Grade 1
- Sight words
- Words to sound out
- Simple sentences

LEVEL 2 — *DEVELOPING READER · 250-750 WORDS*
- Developing Reader
- Grades 1 – 2
- New vocabulary
- Longer sentences

LEVEL 3 — *GROWING READER · 700-1500 WORDS*
- Growing Reader
- Grades 1 – 3
- Reading for inspiration and information

On the back of every book, we have indicated the grade level, guided reading level, Lexile® level, and word count. You can use this information to find a book that is a good fit for your child.

For ideas about sharing books with your new reader, please visit www.scholastic.com. Enjoy helping your child learn to read and love to read!

Happy Reading!

—Francie Alexander
Chief Academic Officer
Scholastic Inc.

ISBN-13: 978-0-545-07078-2
ISBN-10: 0-545-07078-3

12 11 10 9 8 7 6 5 4 3 2 1   9 10 11 12 13 14/0

Printed in the U.S.A.
First printing, March 2009

noodles™

BEGINNING READER
LEVEL 1
50-250 WORDS

NO NEW PETS!

by Hans Wilhelm

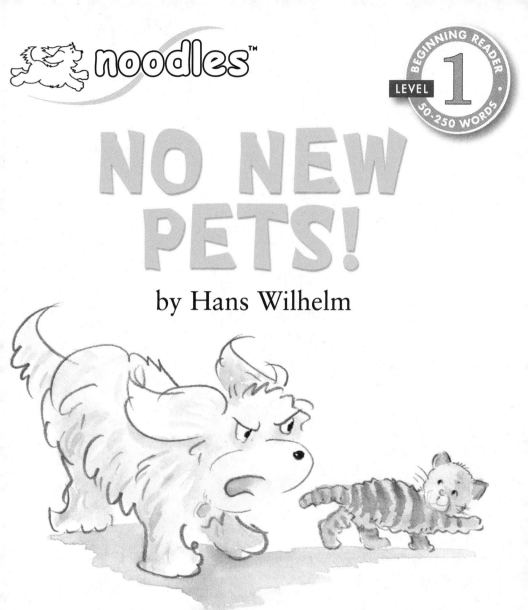

Scholastic Reader — Level 1

SCHOLASTIC INC.

New York   Toronto   London   Auckland   Sydney
Mexico City   New Delhi   Hong Kong   Buenos Aires

What's going on?
She isn't going
to stay, is she?

You don't need her.
You have me!

She won't fetch
sticks for you.

She is too small
to play with.

I'm clever and
I'm cute!
She isn't.

She looks odd.

She walks silly.

She smells funny.

Why would anybody
want her?

Hey, that's *my* Teddy!

I wish she would go away!

Look what a mess
she makes.

What's so funny?

Don't laugh at our kitten!
She is still very small.

She's a tiger kitten.
She'll grow up.
And then she'll eat you
for lunch!

They don't know anything
about little kittens.

Come here.
You can play with
Teddy . . .
for a little while.